Calendar Mysteries

November Night

by Ron Roy

illustrated by
John Steven Gurney

SCHOLASTIC INC.

*I dedicate this book to kind children
who do nice things for other people.*
—R.R.

To Hana and Adelaide
—J.S.G.

No part of this publication may be reproduced, stored in a retrieval system, or
transmitted in any form or by any means, electronic, mechanical, photocopying,
recording, or otherwise, without written permission of the publisher. For
information regarding permission, write to Random House Children's Books,
a division of Random House LLC, a Penguin Random House Company,
1745 Broadway, New York, NY 10019.

ISBN 978-0-545-81212-2

12 11 10 9 8   18 19/0

Printed in the U.S.A.   40

First Scholastic printing, November 2014

November Night

Bradley jumped off his bed and knelt next to Brian. The dead tree was hidden from sight. The neighbors had draped a huge blue tarp around the tree. The tarp hung from the branches all the way to the ground. It was like a big blue tent with the tree inside.

Suddenly a light went on inside the tarp, making it glow. Mr. and Mrs. Sargent were in there. Bradley could see their shapes moving around.

"I don't think they're building a swimming pool," Brian whispered.

"And they're not making a garden, either," Bradley said. "So what *are* they doing?"

"What if Mr. and Mrs. Sargent are spies?" Brian whispered. "Or bank robbers! Maybe they're burying money they stole in their latest robbery! We need to get inside that tarp!"

Contents

1. Spying on the Neighbors 1

2. Bradley's Nightmare 10

3. On the Case 17

4. Weirder and Weirder 26

5. Brian's Great Escape 32

6. Brian's New Plan 42

7. Operation Brian 50

8. Surprise! .58

9. Thanksgiving Friends 67

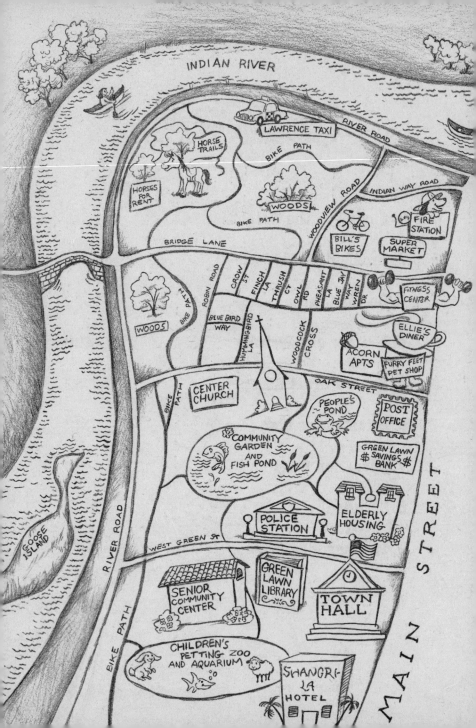

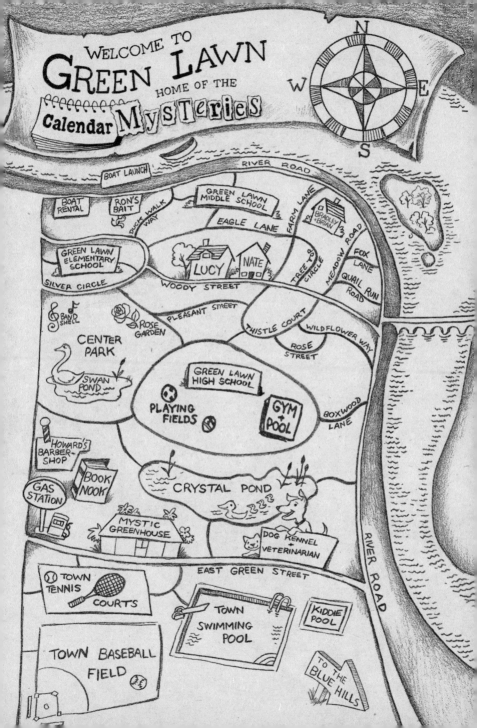

1
Spying on the Neighbors

On the Sunday before Thanksgiving, Bradley Pinto walked into his bedroom. His twin brother, Brian, was kneeling in front of the window. He was peering through binoculars.

"What are you doing?" Bradley asked.

"Nothing," Brian said.

"Yes, you are," Bradley said. "You're spying on the new neighbors again."

"I'm not exactly spying," Brian said. "I'm just checking them out."

Bradley flopped down on his bed. "Mom and Dad gave us the binoculars so we could learn about birds and nature stuff," he said.

"Looking at people is more fun," Brian said. "And I *am* learning about nature. I saw a hawk in the tree."

Bradley knelt next to his brother. He looked at the brand-new fence that surrounded the neighbors' yard. A tall dead tree stood in the middle of the backyard.

Before the new neighbors moved in, the twins used to play inside the tree's hollow trunk. The tree trunk was so big that Bradley and Brian couldn't stretch their arms around it. Sometimes, they would hide in the trunk from their older brother, Josh. Other times, the twins and their friends Nate and Lucy would sit inside and pretend they were lost in the woods. Or they'd pretend to be cave people hiding from ferocious animals.

Bradley had lined the hollow trunk with hay from Polly the pony's stall to make it softer to sit on.

Brian had invented a game called troll in the hole. He would hide inside the tree trunk, wearing a scary Halloween mask. Bradley, Nate, and Lucy would walk past, and Brian would jump out, yelling, "Troll is hungry! Troll is going to eat you!"

Nate would yell, "Don't eat me, Mr. Troll! I taste like rotten eggs!"

Bradley would yell, "Don't eat me, Mr. Troll! I taste like dirty socks!"

Lucy would just run away, laughing.

But last week, a moving van had shown up. Workers unloaded furniture and boxes. New neighbors moved in! Bradley's mom told the twins the neighbors were Mr. and Mrs. Sargent.

A few days later, a truck carrying lumber drove into the driveway. Two men spent a whole day building a tall wood fence around the neighbors' yard with slats so close together that the kids couldn't see through it. There was a wide gate so the Sargents could drive their car inside the fence.

Now the kids couldn't get into the yard. They couldn't play troll in the hole. They could just look at their favorite tree through binoculars.

"Look, there they are!" Brian cried suddenly.

On the other side of the fence were a man and woman. They had gray hair and wore sweaters and jeans. The man had on a red baseball cap. A gray ponytail stuck out the back. They stood and stared up at the old dead tree.

"Maybe they're going to cut the tree down," Bradley said.

"They better not!" Brian wailed. "What about my money?"

"What money?" Bradley asked.

Brian picked up his piggy bank and shook it. The bank was empty. "Every week, I hide my allowance money in a jar. I put the jar inside the old tree under the hay."

Bradley's eyes got wide. "Why do you hide your money?" he asked.

"So Josh won't get it!" Brian said. "He used to sneak in here and borrow money from my bank. Only he forgot to pay it back!"

They both looked out the window. "What if the new neighbors find the jar?" Brian asked. "There's twenty dollars and thirty-seven cents in it!"

"Well, what about my flashlight?" Bradley asked.

"What about it?" Brian said.

"The last time we were playing inside the tree, I left my special flashlight under the hay," Bradley said. "The one with little bats on the handle that glow in the dark!"

Just then, something huge, black, and hairy bolted out of the neighbors' back door. It charged across the yard toward the man and woman.

"Oh my gosh, a bear is attacking Mr. and Mrs. Sargent!" Brian said.

The giant hairy thing stood on its hind legs and began licking Mrs. Sargent's face.

Bradley gulped. "It's just a really big dog," he said. "I guess that's why they built the fence."

The boys' basset hound, Pal, wandered into the room. He padded over to the window and put his front paws on the sill. When he saw the neighbors' dog, he let out a low growl.

Brian patted Pal on his head. "Don't worry, boy," he said. "We'll protect you!"

Pal ran and hid under Bradley's bed.

The boys watched the neighbors walk into their garage. They came out lugging a long ladder. They leaned the ladder against the tree.

Mr. Sargent climbed up into the tree.

He unclipped a tape measure from his belt and measured the lowest branches. Mrs. Sargent wrote something on a clipboard pad. Then she unrolled a big sheet of paper. She spread it out on the ground and put rocks on the corners. Her husband came down, and they got on their

knees and studied the unrolled paper. Mrs. Sargent wrote more things on her pad.

Brian trained the binoculars onto the paper. "It's all funny drawings," he said. "Grandpa had pictures like that when he built his boat, remember?"

"Do you think they're going to build a boat?" Bradley asked.

"I don't care what they build as long as they don't cut our tree down!"

"Um, it's not our tree," Bradley said. "It's their tree now."

The boys watched the neighbors walk all around the tree. Mr. Sargent took more measurements. Mrs. Sargent wrote more things on her pad.

Mr. Sargent put his head inside the hollow part of the tree. He crawled inside, then came out again. He said something to his wife, and they both laughed. They went back to the pictures on the roll of paper. They scratched their heads.

"Don't look under the hay!" Bradley whispered.

Mr. Sargent went into the house and came out with two mugs. Bradley could see the steam rising. The neighbors sipped from their mugs and stared at their tree. They sat on the ground and leaned against the trunk.

The twins heard their mother's voice from downstairs. "Supper, you two!" she called. "And wash your hands, please."

2
Bradley's Nightmare

"You guys were pretty quiet in your room," their father said. "Were you hatching some evil plan?" He grinned.

"No, but we think the new neighbors are going to build something in their backyard," Bradley said. "They might cut the tree down!"

"How do you know?" their mother asked. She passed a plate full of fried chicken.

"Brian is spying on them with the binoculars," Bradley said.

"Mr. and Mrs. Sargent are from Florida," the boys' father said, passing the green beans to Josh. "A lot of people in Florida have swimming pools in their yards. Maybe the Sargents are going to put in a swimming pool."

"Sweet!" Josh said. "They could hire me to keep it clean."

"I'll bet they're going to plant a vegetable garden," Mrs. Pinto said. "I think Martha Sargent misses her garden in Florida."

"Mom, it's almost Thanksgiving," Bradley said. "Why would she plant a garden now?"

"You're right, honey," his mom said. "I meant in the springtime."

"Good, maybe she'll give us some of her vegetables," Mr. Pinto said.

"No way!" Josh said. "We don't need more vegetables in this house. Mom makes us eat too many already. One of these days, I'm going to turn green!"

"Like Kermit the Frog," Bradley said, grinning at Josh.

"I should invite them over for a meal," their mother said. "I think Martha and Ralph miss their kids and grandkids."

"Just don't invite their dog," Josh said. "He'd eat *us*!"

After supper, Bradley and Brian went upstairs. Brian stepped into the bathroom, and Bradley went into their bedroom and picked up his book.

"I can't wait for Thanksgiving," he said. "Only a few more days!"

"Me too," Brian said. He came out of the bathroom, wiping toothpaste off his chin. "Pumpkin pie! Ice cream! Mashed potatoes!"

He knelt in front of the window and looked outside. "Oh my gosh! Bradley, come and see!"

Bradley jumped off his bed and knelt next to Brian. The dead tree was hidden from sight. The neighbors had draped a huge blue tarp around the tree. The tarp hung from the branches all the way to the ground. It was like a big blue tent with the tree inside.

Suddenly a light went on inside the tarp, making it glow. Mr. and Mrs. Sargent were in there. Bradley could see their shapes moving around.

"I don't think they're building a swimming pool," Brian whispered.

"And they're not making a garden, either," Bradley said. "So what *are* they doing?"

"What if Mr. and Mrs. Sargent are spies?" Brian whispered. "Or bank robbers! Maybe they're burying money they stole in their latest robbery! We need to get inside that tarp!"

"We?" Bradley said.

"Yeah, you, me, Lucy, and Nate," Brian said. "Let's call them!"

Lucy Armstrong was the cousin of Josh's friend Dink. She was staying with Dink's family for a year while her parents worked on a Native American reservation in Arizona.

Nate's older sister, Ruth Rose, was Josh's other best friend. His family lived next door to Dink, so all the kids were friends.

Bradley looked at the clock. "It's too late to call," he said. "But we'll see them tomorrow morning at school." He changed into his pajamas.

"There is something weird about our new neighbors," Brian said. "And we're going to find out what!"

Bradley fell asleep thinking about what could be going on inside the strange blue tarp. He dreamed that he was climbing over the fence to get a closer look. Suddenly the giant black dog appeared out of the night. It leaped on Bradley and started to—

Bradley woke up screaming.

"It's only a nightmare," he whispered to himself. But it had seemed so real! Bradley closed his eyes and thought about Thanksgiving pumpkin pie and ice cream. Finally, he went back to sleep.

3
On the Case

At eight-thirty the next morning, Bradley and Brian met their two friends on the corner of Farm Lane and Woody Street. They always walked to school with Nate and Lucy.

"Our new neighbors are doing something strange next door!" Brian blurted out.

"Like what?" Nate asked.

"You know our favorite tree?" Brian asked. "They measured it, then covered it with this blue tarp thing. And they're doing something inside the tarp, where we can't see them! All we could see was their shadows."

"Maybe they're digging for treasure," Lucy said.

"They have a giant dog," Bradley said. "About ten times as big as Pal!" He told them about his nightmare.

"Yeah, and Bradley screamed so loud I woke up!" Brian added.

The kids hurried toward the elementary school.

"I wish I was invisible," Brian said. "Then I could climb over the fence and that big old dog wouldn't even see me!"

"But he'd still smell you," Nate said. "Then he'd follow his nose and gobble you up!"

Bradley grinned. "Maybe if you put on some of Mom's perfume, the dog would think you were a rosebush!"

"Very funny," Brian said.

They reached their school as the bell

was ringing. "We need to investigate," Brian said. "Can you come to our house right after school?"

"Sure," Lucy said. "I love solving mysteries!"

"Me too," Nate said. "But I'm not wearing any perfume!"

At three o'clock, the four kids ran back to Bradley and Brian's house on Farm Lane.

Above the backyard fence, they could see the blue tarp hanging from the tree's branches.

"I wonder if they're home," Bradley whispered.

Lucy found a knothole in the fence. "Nobody's there," she whispered. "But I can see their green car in the driveway."

"Can you see the dog?" Brian asked.

Lucy shook her head. "Nope, just a squirrel."

They each took a turn peeking

through the hole. "Guys, the Sargents are coming out of their house!" Nate said. "They're walking toward the car."

Nate looked at Bradley. "They don't look weird to me."

Brian put his eye to the hole. "Shhh, they're talking!" he whispered. "Mrs. Sargent said they're going shopping in town."

The other three kids placed their

ears against the fence. They all heard car doors slamming.

Brian was still looking through the knothole. "And Mrs. Sargent has her clipboard. She was making a list yesterday."

"Yeah," Bradley said. "I bet if we follow them, we can find out what they buy. Then we can figure out what they're doing!"

"Wait!" Brian said. "After they leave,

I can sneak over and get my jar of money!" He had told Nate and Lucy about hiding his allowance in the old tree.

"And my flashlight," Bradley added.

"What about the dog?" Nate asked.

Brian peeked through the knothole again. "Rats," he said. "The dog is sleeping under the tree!"

"Let's go to Main Street," Bradley said. "If we get there before they do, we can spy on them!"

The kids took off running. They raced down Eagle Lane, then cut through the playground at the elementary school. A few minutes later, they were on Main Street, across from the fire station.

"Stop! I have a pain in my side from running!" Nate said. He bent over and held his side.

"There they are!" Bradley said. The neighbors' green car was at the stop sign on Silver Circle. Then it turned onto Main Street. Bradley could see Mr.

Sargent driving. Mrs. Sargent sat next to him. The car pulled into the supermarket parking lot.

The kids crossed Main Street and ran to the back of the fire station. Its parking lot was next to the supermarket lot. The kids arrived just in time to see the green car turn into a space and stop.

"Are they going grocery shopping?" Nate asked.

Bradley, Brian, Nate, and Lucy were hiding behind a row of bushes. They watched Mr. and Mrs. Sargent leave their car and head to the rear of the supermarket. She was carrying the clipboard.

"They might be going to that little hardware store inside the supermarket," Brian said.

"Should we follow them?" Bradley asked.

"They'll spot us if we do," Brian said. "They must have seen us next door."

"I can go in," Lucy said. "They don't know me! Come with me, Nate."

"Good idea," Bradley said. "Find out what they buy!"

He and Brian watched Lucy and Nate scoot between some cars. They slipped into the supermarket's back door two minutes behind Mr. and Mrs. Sargent.

"I'll be right back," Bradley told Brian. He ran to the neighbors' car and peeked into the back. He saw an old blanket, a bunch of tools, and a map of Florida.

"Bradley! Come on!" Brian called. Bradley ran back to his brother. Mr. and Mrs. Sargent came out carrying bags. They headed right for their car.

The bags were lumpy. They looked heavy.

Just then, Nate and Lucy ran up to the twins.

"We got it!" Lucy said.

"Got what?" Brian asked.

"This!" Lucy said. She held out a receipt. "I saw Mr. Sargent drop this into the trash, so I grabbed it!"

The four kids huddled together and read what was on the receipt:

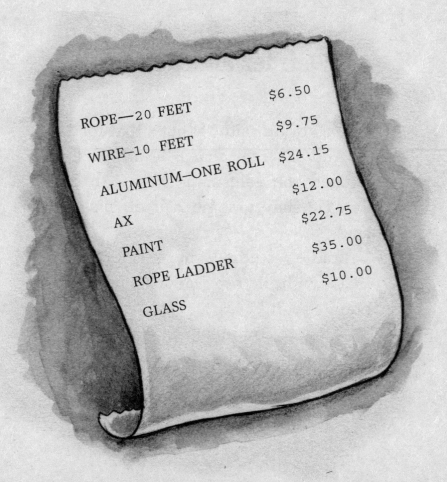

ROPE—20 FEET $6.50
WIRE—10 FEET $9.75
ALUMINUM—ONE ROLL $24.15
AX $12.00
PAINT $22.75
ROPE LADDER $35.00
GLASS $10.00

4
Weirder and Weirder

"An ax!" Brian said. "What's that for?"

"And it's real sharp!" Nate said. "I watched the salesman show Mr. Sargent. He shaved some hair off his own arm!"

Bradley studied the receipt. "And what's with the rope ladder?" he asked. "I don't get it."

"They're coming back!" Lucy said.

Mr. and Mrs. Sargent walked past the kids' hiding spot. Now they weren't carrying anything except the clipboard.

"They must have put the stuff in their car," Bradley said.

"Where are they going now?" Nate asked.

"Let's follow them," Brian said.

The four kids fell in behind Mr. and Mrs. Sargent. The couple walked into the gas station, and the kids hid behind some bushes. They had a perfect view of their neighbors as they chatted with Mr. Holly, the owner.

They watched Mr. Holly pull something off a shelf and hand it to Mr. Sargent.

"What is it?" Brian whispered.

"I don't know," Lucy said.

"I'll find out!" Nate said. He dashed up to a window. Nate was only six feet away from the Sargents and Mr. Holly.

A minute later, he came racing back. "It's some kind of motor," he said. "He's telling them how it runs."

"An ax and a rope ladder and a motor?" Bradley said. "Very weird!"

"Watch out. Here they come!" Lucy said.

The four spies ducked as the Sargents strolled past them. Mr. Sargent carried a box.

The kids followed, tiptoeing and silent.

Bradley tried to figure out what the Sargents could be building that needed a motor. A submarine? A car? An airplane?

The Sargents left the motor in their car, then walked up Bridge Lane to Bill's Bikes. The kids heard a little bell jingle as the neighbors stepped inside Bill's door.

"Maybe they're buying a bike," Nate said.

"They have a plan," Bradley said. "We just don't know what it is. But do you think they bought the ax to cut down that tree?"

"I don't think they can cut down that huge tree with an ax," Lucy said. "It would take them a year!"

"I hope you're right," Bradley said. Then the door of Bill's Bikes opened with another jingle. Mr. and Mrs. Sargent came out, carrying two large bags. Once again, they headed for their car.

"I wonder what's in those bags," Brian whispered.

"I'll find out!" Bradley said. He ran up to Bill's and entered the shop. The jingling bell sounded again.

Bill smiled at Bradley. "Hey, what's up?" he asked.

Bradley went over to the counter. Bill was squirting oil onto a bike chain. "You know that couple who were just in here?" he asked.

"Yep, Mr. and Mrs. Sargent. Real nice people," Bill said. "They told me they just moved up here from Florida."

"They bought the house next to ours," Bradley informed Bill. "And they're building something in the backyard. My friends and my brother and I are trying to figure out what it is."

Bill raised his eyebrows. "Why do you want to know?" he asked.

"We're playing detectives," Bradley

said. "It's kind of a mystery and we're looking for clues."

Bill grinned. "They bought a bunch of bike parts: couple of seats, some chains, and half a dozen pedals," he said.

"Do you think they're building bikes?" Bradley asked.

Bill laughed. "That's what I asked them," he said. "They told me they were working on a secret project."

Bradley thanked Bill and hurried out the door. He ran back to the other kids. "They bought bike parts," he said. *"For a secret project!"*

"Weirder and weirder," Brian said.

"There they go," Nate said. They all watched the green car pull out of the parking lot.

5
Brian's Great Escape

The kids ran back to the twins' house. Bradley peeked through the knothole in the fence. He didn't see the neighbors or their car. But the big black dog was lying under the tree with his eyes closed.

"They're not home yet," Bradley said.

"Running makes me hungry. Let's go in and get a snack," Brian said.

They trooped into the house, where they found a bowl of apples on the kitchen table. They each took one and went back outside. Brian walked over to the knothole. "Monster Dog is still sleeping," he told the other kids.

"I wonder what his name is," Bradley said.

"Probably something like *Killer*," Nate said.

Brian knocked on the fence. "Here, Killer," he called. "Good Killer, come and say hello."

Suddenly the giant dog leaped up and charged the fence. He stood on his hind legs, put his paws on the wood, and barked. His long pink tongue came through the knothole.

Bradley leaped backward. "It's just like in my nightmare!" he said.

Brian jumped, too, dropping his apple. It rolled in the dirt. "Rats," he said.

He held the dirty apple up to the knothole. "Do you like apples, Killer?" he asked the dog.

The tongue came through the knot-hole again. Brian let the dog lick the apple, and then he tossed it over the fence. They all heard the dog begin to chew.

"I guess Killer likes fruit," Lucy said.

"This gives me an idea!" Brian said. "We can get him away from the tree with our apples! Then, when he's busy eating, I can go over the fence and get my money and Bradley's flashlight."

Brian pointed at some bushes at the far end of the fence. "If we can get him to the other side of those bushes, he won't be able to see me climb over," he said.

"But he might smell you!" Lucy said.

"You'll be his Brian burger!" Nate put in.

"Don't do it," Bradley said.

"But don't you guys want to know what they're doing behind that tarp?" Brian asked. He lowered his voice. "They could be burying a dead body! We could turn them in to Officer Fallon. We'd be heroes!"

"How will you get over the fence?" Nate asked. He reached up, and his hand didn't quite touch the top of the fence. "It's about five feet tall."

"Why wouldn't you just go through the gate where they bring their car in?" Lucy asked.

"Can't," Brian said. "It's latched on the inside. But I can use Dad's new ladder. Help me get it, Bradley!" He and Bradley ran toward the barn.

Josh, Bradley, and Brian had bought their dad a shiny new aluminum ladder for his birthday. The twins came back carrying the six-foot ladder. They leaned it against the fence. "I can jump down on the other side," Brian said.

"But then how will you come back?" Lucy asked. "The ladder will be on our side of the fence."

"I didn't think about that," Brian said.

"I know!" Nate said. "Lucy will go to the corner of the fence with our apples. The dog will smell them and follow her. Bradley and I will stay here with Brian. After he goes over, Bradley and I will lift the ladder over the fence. And that's how Brian will get back into this yard."

"Excellent plan!" Brian said. "Okay, Lucy, do your stuff!"

"One teensy problem," Bradley said. "How will we get Dad's ladder back on this side again?"

"We'll figure that out later," Brian said.

Bradley and Nate handed Lucy their partly eaten apples. Lucy ran toward Meadow Road, where the fence turned a corner. She made sure she was past the bushes. Then she banged on the fence. "Here, doggy! Here, Killer!" Lucy called. "Lucy has yummy apples for you!"

Brian, Bradley, and Nate were still at the knothole. "It worked!" Nate yelled. "Killer's running toward Lucy!"

Bradley and Nate held the ladder while Brian scrambled up. At the top, he looked toward where he could hear Killer gobbling up the apples. Because of the bushes, the dog couldn't see him.

Brian jumped into the neighbors'

yard. "Send the ladder over!" he yelled through the fence.

Bradley and Nate hoisted the ladder up and shoved it. They heard it drop onto the neighbors' lawn.

Bradley stuck his eye to the knot-hole. He saw Brian heading for the blue tarp at the same time that Lucy yelled, "The green car is coming!" She raced toward Bradley and Nate. "Your neighbors are back!"

Bradley put his mouth to the knot-hole and shouted, "Brian, the neighbors are coming! Escape, dude!"

They heard car doors slamming.

They heard Killer barking with happiness.

Just then, the top of the ladder appeared over the fence. Brian came next, practically flying over. He landed on the ground at Bradley's feet.

Brian's face was red, but he was

grinning. "That was close!" he said. He rubbed his arm. "Skinned the heck out of my elbow!"

"But where's your money jar?" Bradley asked his twin. "And my flashlight?"

Brian got up and brushed off his pants. "I didn't have time to get to the tree," he said. "Sorry, bro."

Nate was looking through the knothole. "The car is inside the gate now!" he whispered.

The dog was barking like mad.

"Get Dad's ladder!" Bradley said.

"How?" Brian said. "I can't reach it!" He grabbed his brother's arm and started to run.

The four kids raced into the barn. They flopped down on a pile of hay outside Polly's stall. The pony looked over her stall door and made a funny noise with her lips.

Bradley reached into the stall and

patted Polly on her nose. "Now the neighbors have your money, my flashlight, and Dad's birthday ladder," he said.

"They have something else," Brian added. "I saw about twenty bags of cement piled up behind the blue tarp. And a bunch of long iron pipes."

6
Brian's New Plan

"Cement and iron?" Bradley said. "Maybe they're building a cage for Killer."

"But why would they buy a rope ladder and bike parts?" Lucy asked.

Brian opened his eyes wide and made a zombie face. *The Killer Dog Mystery!* he said in a spooky voice.

Bradley tossed some hay at his brother. "You won't think it's so funny when Dad comes out here looking for his new ladder," he said.

Just then, they heard a loud buzzing sound.

"That's coming from their yard!" Bradley said.

"What the heck is that?" Nate asked. "It sounds like an airplane!"

"It's a chain saw," Lucy said. "My dad has one. He uses it to cut down trees."

"Oh no!" Brian said. "How will we get our things back if they cut the tree down?"

Five minutes later, the buzzing noise stopped. The kids ran back to the fence. Lucy got to the knothole first. "I can see the tarp and the dog," she said. "No people. No chain saw."

"We need a plan," Brian said.

"We *had* a plan," Bradley said.

"And it would have worked if the neighbors hadn't come back so soon," Brian said.

"And if their dog wasn't a giant monster!" Bradley said.

"In the movies, the burglars feed the guard dogs sleeping pills," Nate said. "When they fall asleep, the burglars walk right past them!"

Brian grinned. "We don't have sleeping pills," he said. "But you gave me an awesome idea, Nate. I can sneak over there when the Sargents and Killer are asleep!"

"How are you going to get over the fence?" Bradley asked. "Dad's ladder is still on their side, remember? And the gate will be locked."

"Easy," Brian said. "You three will boost me over. Then I'll unlatch the gate, and you guys can come in. We'll grab Dad's ladder and my money jar and run back home. Cinchy!"

"And my flashlight!" Bradley said.

"It will be in the papers tomorrow," Nate said. He closed his eyes and said, "Killer Dog Eats Redheaded Boy."

"Not to worry," Brian said. "I can outrun that big old dog."

"I like your plan," Lucy said. "When can we do it?"

"How about Wednesday night?" Brian said. "Your families are all coming to our house. We'll get permission for you guys to sleep over. At midnight, we'll sneak out. It'll be fun!"

Nate opened his eyes wide. "Creeping around in the dark with a killer dog on the loose doesn't sound like fun!" he said.

Brian stood. "Operation Brian is a perfect plan," he said. "Nothing will go wrong."

Bradley laughed. "Gee, sneaking past Mom and Dad's bedroom, climbing over a fence in the dark, fighting off a monster dog—what could possibly go wrong?"

Brian grinned. "Trust me," he said.

During school recess the next day, the four kids talked about Operation Brian.

"We should all wear dark clothes," Brian said. "Like ninjas."

"I still think it's crazy," Nate said. "That dog is gigantic!"

"I sure hope Mom and Dad don't wake up and catch us," Bradley said.

The next day was Wednesday. Nate's family came to Bradley's house for dinner at six-thirty. Lucy and Dink's family showed up a few minutes later. Nate and Lucy had permission to sleep over. They each brought a sleeping bag. Hidden inside the sleeping bags were their dark clothes.

Thirteen people sat down to eat supper. Dink, Josh, and Ruth Rose were excited about Thanksgiving the next day.

Bradley, Brian, Nate, and Lucy were excited about Operation Brian. It was only five hours away.

After supper, everyone played board games. The kids played Scrabble. Nate went first, and he made DOG as his word.

"Did you see our new neighbors' dog?" Josh asked Dink and Ruth Rose. "He's the biggest monster I've ever seen!"

Bradley poked Brian, Nate, and Lucy under the table. They all grinned.

At ten o'clock, the Duncans and Hathaways thanked the Pintos for supper and went home. Nate and Lucy followed the twins upstairs to their room and unrolled their sleeping bags under the window.

Next door, the tarp glowed from the light inside.

The kids saw shapes moving around behind the tarp.

They heard sanding noises and scraping noises and hammering noises and chain-saw noises.

They heard Mr. and Mrs. Sargent laughing.

"They're working on their secret project," Lucy said.

"What could it be?" Nate asked.

"We'll know pretty soon," Brian said.

"If your plan works," Nate said.

"Operation Brian will totally work," Brian declared. "In two hours, we'll know what's going on inside that blue tarp. And we'll have Dad's ladder, my money, and Bradley's flashlight."

Their dad's voice came from downstairs: "Go to sleep! Not a peep! Or up the stairs I'll creep!"

Lucy giggled. "Your dad is so funny!"

"Not if he catches us sneaking out," Bradley said.

The four kids pulled on their dark clothes.

The twins got into their beds, and Nate and Lucy crawled into their sleeping bags.

Bradley shut off the light.

"How will we know when it's midnight?" Nate asked.

"I'll wake you," Brian said. "I've got the clock in bed with me so Mom, Dad, and Josh won't hear the alarm. I set it for twelve o'clock."

"This will be so exciting!" Lucy said. "I've never snuck out in the middle of the night before!"

7

Operation Brian

Bradley woke up to more strange noises. He turned to look at his clock. It was gone. Then he remembered that Brian had it in his bed.

Bradley heard car doors slamming. He heard people talking outside. It sounded like more than two people, and they were giggling. Who would be laughing outside in the dark? he wondered.

Then Bradley heard a dog barking. It was a big bark from a big dog. *What's Killer the dog doing outside in the mid-*

dle of the night? Bradley wondered. *If Killer sleeps outdoors tonight, Brian's plan is doomed!*

That was Bradley's last thought before he went back to sleep.

Suddenly he heard a soft ringing noise. Ten seconds later, something grabbed his arm. He lunged up and yelled, "AHHHH!"

"Quiet—you'll wake Mom and Dad!" Brian whispered. "Come on. It's time for OB."

"What's OB?" Nate asked from his sleeping bag.

"Operation Brian!" Brian whispered. "Get up."

"Is it midnight already?" Lucy asked. She crawled out of her sleeping bag. Yawning, she pushed her long blond hair out of her eyes.

The kids tugged on their sneakers in the dark.

"Brian, I heard their dog barking," Bradley whispered. "I think Killer is outside!"

Brian looked at Bradley. "When did you hear him?" he asked. "He's not barking now."

"A while ago," Bradley said. "When I was sleeping, but I woke up, I think."

Brian grinned. "You were having one

of your famous nightmares," he said. "You guys ready? Come on!"

With Brian leading, they tiptoed down the hall.

They went past Brian and Bradley's parents' room, then the bathroom. They passed Josh's room. Bradley noticed light under his door. *Why is Josh still awake?* he wondered.

They went down the stairs.

Through the kitchen, where Brian grabbed another apple.

Out the door.

Operation Brian was working!

The kids crept across the backyard. The moon was nearly full, lighting the way to the fence. Their sneakers made no sounds on the soft grass.

Bradley put his eye to the knothole. "Nothing moving," he reported.

"Can you see Killer?" Brian asked.

Bradley looked again. "Nope, just the big blue tarp," he said. "But he could be out there somewhere."

"That's why I brought this," Brian said. He tossed the apple over the fence, then put his eye to the knothole. "No noise, no dog. So now you guys can boost me up, like they do in the Boy Scouts."

"I'm not a Boy Scout," Lucy said.

"I'm not even a Cub Scout," Nate added.

"Josh taught me this," Brian said. He told Nate and Lucy to squat down. He showed them how to make a seat by crisscrossing their hands and arms. When they were ready, Brian put one foot on top of their joined hands. He balanced by holding on to Bradley's head.

Nate and Lucy stood up, slowly lifting Brian.

"You're heavy," Nate grunted.

"You're pulling my hair!" Bradley said.

Brian grabbed the top of the fence. "A little higher!" he said.

Bradley shoved his brother's rear end.

"Okay, I'm up!" Brian said. "Go to the gate, and I'll let you in!"

"Unless Killer eats you first!" Nate said.

Brian grinned in the moonlight. "Killer is in the house dreaming doggy dreams," he said. Then he dropped out

of sight into the neighbors' yard.

Bradley, Nate, and Lucy raced toward the gate.

When they got there, Brian was shoving it open. "Come on in," he whispered. "And be quiet!"

Single file, they followed Brian across the yard. In the moonlight, the tarp was a tall blue ghost. The green car sat in the driveway. Bradley thought it looked like a crouching dragon. Moonlight made the car's headlights gleam like eyes.

Suddenly the house lit up.

A light went on inside the tarp.

The yard was filled with bright light, as if it were noon instead of midnight. Then the neighbors' back door opened. Killer came bounding out, barking like crazy.

He charged across the yard, straight toward Bradley.

8
Surprise!

Killer barked like a maniac. His eyes and teeth shone in the moonlight. He reared up on his hind legs and slammed his giant front paws into Bradley's chest.

My nightmare is coming true! Bradley thought as he landed on his back on the grass. One hundred pounds of hairy black dog piled on top of him. A huge pink tongue washed his face. Bradley was too scared to yell.

"Daisy, get off!" a voice shouted.

Bradley looked up. He saw a boy tugging on the dog's collar. Then a girl was there, and she was tugging, too. They both had brown hair. They looked about ten years old.

Finally, Daisy got off, and Bradley looked up. Brian, Nate, and Lucy were standing with Bradley's parents, who were wearing bathrobes. Josh was there, too, wearing sweatpants, a hoodie, and a silly grin.

Suddenly Pal raced through the gate, into the crowd. He and Daisy sniffed each other, then began racing around the yard, playing doggy tag.

"What're you guys doing here?" Bradley asked his family.

"A better question," his dad said, "is what are *you* doing here?"

Josh helped Bradley up off the ground. The two new kids were standing next to the neighbors.

"These are our grandchildren from

Florida," Mrs. Sargent said. "Charlie and Maddy."

Everyone said hi.

"It's cold out here," Mr. Sargent said. "Let's go inside."

Eleven people crowded into the neighbors' kitchen.

"Find your seat, everyone," Mrs. Sargent said. "The hot chocolate is almost ready."

Bradley blinked under a bright light. A long table was set with eleven places. There were eleven mugs, eleven napkins, eleven spoons. A plate of cookies sat in the middle of the table. The cookies were shaped like turkeys, with raisins for eyes.

On each place mat was a cardboard-turkey name tag. Bradley found his name and sat down. Then he laughed. Standing next to his mug was his flashlight!

Next to him, Brian laughed, too.
There was his jar of money.

They knew we were coming! Bradley
said to himself.

Soon everyone began sipping from

the mugs and munching on cookies.

"How did you know about Operation Brian?" Brian asked.

"A little birdie told us," Mr. Sargent said. "So we knew you were curious about what was going on under our tarp."

"The same little birdie told us your plan about sneaking over here tonight," Bradley's mother said.

"What little birdie?" Bradley asked.

Josh grinned and patted himself on the chest. "Tweet, tweet!" he said. "I heard you guys talking in your room. You should keep your door closed!"

"We had fun sitting in the dark and watching you sneak into the yard," Mrs. Sargent said.

"And I heard you creeping past my door," Josh said. "You were about as quiet as a herd of elephants!"

"So I nearly broke my neck for nothing!" Brian said.

"And I got attacked by a giant dog for nothing!" Bradley said.

"Daisy wouldn't hurt a fly," Maddy said. "She just wanted to kiss you."

"If you had asked, we would have told you," Mrs. Sargent said. "We're building a special Thanksgiving surprise for Charlie and Maddy."

"Granddad, what is it?" Charlie asked. "I can't wait till tomorrow!"

Mr. Sargent stood up and looked at his watch. "Well, since it's almost one in the morning, it's officially Thanksgiving Day," he said. "Let's go take a look!"

Charlie and Maddy raced out the door. Bradley, Brian, Nate, and Lucy ran after them.

Everyone gathered in front of the blue tarp. Mrs. Sargent tugged on a rope, and the tarp fell to the ground.

The "surprise" was tall and silver and shiny. It gleamed in the moonlight.

"It's a space shuttle!" Maddy shouted.

"Thank you, Grandpa and Grandma!"

"Charlie and Maddy live near the Kennedy Space Center in Florida," Mrs. Sargent explained. "They love to go there and see the launches. So we decided to build them their own shuttle in our backyard!"

"But where's the tree?" Bradley asked.

"It's inside," Mr. Sargent said. "We cut off most of the branches and used some of the wood inside the shuttle. The tree is very old, so we used cement and steel bars to make it stronger."

The spaceship was made of aluminum that covered the tree, and light shone through round windows. There was a door to go inside.

"It's wonderful!" Bradley's mother said. "What clever new neighbors we have!"

"Can we go in it?" Nate asked.

"Of course," Mr. Sargent said.

The kids opened the door and stepped inside, where Bradley and Brian used to play. The wood from the tree branches had been turned into seats. A rope ladder hung from the top. One by one, the kids climbed the ladder. It led to a platform where they could sit on pillows.

Sticking up from the floor were a bike seat and two pedals attached to a chain. The chain was hooked up to a small motor.

Charlie sat on the bike seat, put his feet on the pedals, and pushed down. Suddenly one of the windows turned into a TV screen. At first, it was black, but then the kids saw planets and stars appear.

"Awesome!" Nate said. "I feel like an astronaut!"

9
Thanksgiving Friends

Everyone got a chance to go inside the space shuttle. Finally, the kids began to yawn. "Okay, it's time to call it a night," Bradley's father said. "Happy Thanksgiving, everyone!"

Bradley, Brian, Nate, and Lucy went back to the twins' room. Within minutes, they were all asleep.

On Thanksgiving morning, a loud barking woke Bradley. He crawled over Nate's sleeping bag and looked down at the ground. On the other side of the fence, Daisy was barking. Pal was sitting on his side of the fence, barking right back!

Brian woke up and looked out the window.

Mr. Pinto and Mr. Sargent were standing by the fence, talking. Mr. Sargent was holding his chain saw.

Nate sat up. "What's going on?" he asked.

"My dad and Mr. Sargent are out there talking," Bradley said.

Lucy's head popped up. She rested her chin on the sill and looked down.

Suddenly Mr. Sargent started the chain saw. He began cutting the fence. In two minutes, there was a big space where a section of the fence had fallen to the ground.

Pal raced into the Sargents' yard. He and Daisy began chasing each other.

"Oh my gosh, there's a big hole in the fence!" Bradley said.

"Charlie and Maddy are already playing in the shuttle!" Brian said.

The four kids ran downstairs and dashed outside. Charlie and Maddy waved to them. "Come on up!" they yelled.

The cutout section of fence was lying on the grass. Mr. Sargent was measuring it with his shiny tape. "I can make a nifty gate out of this wood," he said.

"I think I've got some hinges in the barn," Bradley's father said.

"What're you doing, Dad?" Bradley asked his father.

"Our new neighbor decided there should be a gate here," Mr. Pinto said.

Mr. Sargent smiled. "Our grandkids will be leaving soon, and we want *you* kids to play in the space shuttle while they're gone," he said. "The gate will always be unlocked for you."

Mrs. Sargent poked her head out the back door. "What's all the racket?" she asked.

"Grandpa cut part of the fence down!" Charlie said.

"Oh, what a marvelous idea!" Mrs. Sargent said. "Now it will be so much easier to get to know our new friends!"

Bradley's mother opened her back door. "Everyone come over for juice and muffins!" she called across the yard.

Charlie and Maddy came down, and they all walked through the hole where the fence once stood.

Bradley whispered to his mother, "Mom, can we invite everyone over for Thanksgiving dinner?"

His mother smiled. "I already asked them," she whispered back. "Now I just have to figure out where to get a bigger table!"

Jennifer Crusie

National bestselling author of
Fast Women and *Welcome to Temptation*

DBP244463

GETTING
RID OF
BRADLEY

Some men are just harder to get rid of....

MIRA
$5.99 U. S.
$6.99 CAN.

Also available from bestselling author

Jennifer Crusie

and **MIRA®** Books

Jennifer Crusie

National bestselling author of *Crazy for You*
and *Welcome to Temptation*

MAN HUNTING

A wickedly funny tale about one woman's best-laid plans...

ISBN 1-55166-865-3

"Nobody's trying to kill me," Lucy said, trying to sound reasonably calm. "Get off."

"So you're telling me I overreacted." The warmth in his eyes went to her bones, and she swallowed hard.

"I forgive you. Now, get off me."

"You know, in this light, your hair looks sort of...green."

"Get off me now!"

The car blew up.

"Zack!" Lucy threw her arms around him and pulled him down to her. After a moment of silence, Zack raised his shoulders off Lucy and gazed cautiously over the hill at her burning car.

"Nice little bomb," he said reflectively. "Very neat."

Lucy eased the top of her body up, too, still under him, and watched the flames, horrified. He looked down at her, and when she turned back they were nose-to-nose.

"You okay?"

"Zack," Lucy said. "Somebody's trying to kill me."

"You know," Zack said, "I had an instinct about that."

Also available from MIRA Books and
JENNIFER CRUSIE

MANHUNTING

Coming soon
WHAT THE LADY WANTS
November 2002

Jennifer Crusie

GETTING RID OF BRADLEY

MIRA

ISBN 1-55166-865-3

GETTING RID OF BRADLEY

Copyright © 1994 by Jennifer Crusie.

Visit us at www.mirabooks.com

Printed in U.S.A.